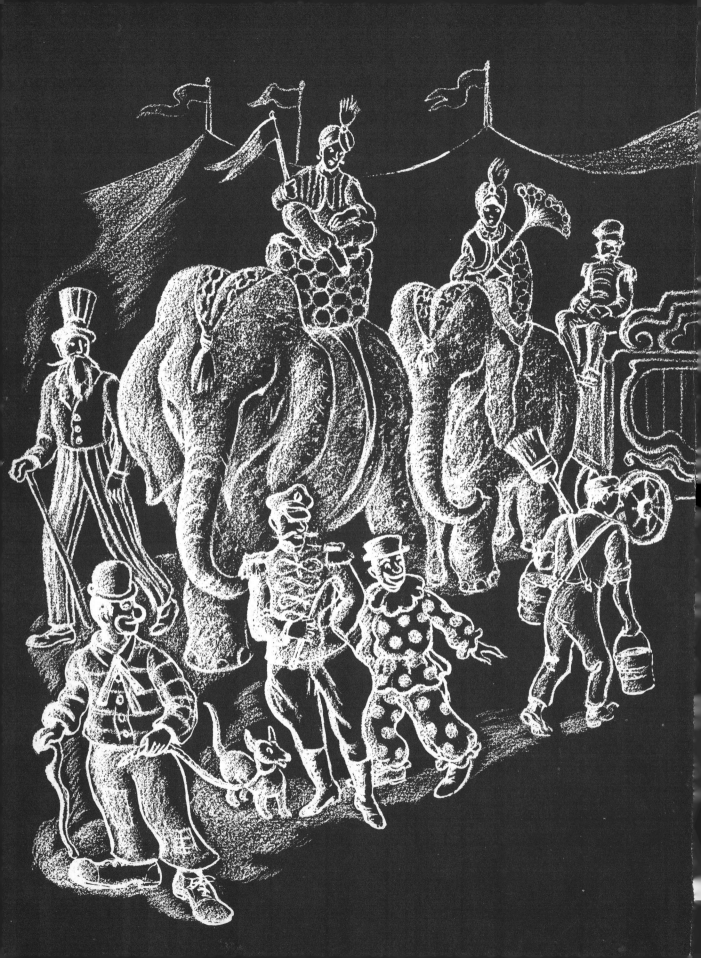

GREATEST SHOW ON EART

Andy and the Circus

ANDY
and the
CIRCUS

**Written and Illustrated
by
Ellis Credle**

Thomas Nelson Inc.
New York   Camden

For Michael

who rode the bike

First U.S. edition

Library of Congress Catalog Card Number: 74-164968
International Standard Book Number: 0-8407-6164-3
                               0-8407-6165-1 NLB
Printed in the United States of America

45356

Andy and the Circus

It was a hot afternoon. Andy had been to town to do some errands. He had a block of ice for his mother's old ice chest and a heavy iron point for his father's plow. In his pocket was a little bag of horehound candy for Grandpa. He was pedaling home, pushing hard, when he came upon a circus poster. Andy braked his bike and stood looking.

Oh, what a picture! Up high, men and women were flying from swing to swing. Monkeys pedaled bicycles on a high wire. And the clowns, oh, the clowns! Everywhere there were clowns doing funny tricks.

"Oh, what fun to be a clown," Andy thought. "To be in the circus doing funny tricks! What fun to sleep on a train, wake up in a new town every morning, to be a clown in the big show!" He could have stayed all day looking, but the ice was melting. He had to shove on.

Along the road was Joe's house, and there was Joe running down the walk. He was holding a big basket.

"Wait a minute, Andy," Joe cried. "I want to show you what I've got!" He held out the basket.

Andy stopped. He leaned over and peered. The box was
full of kittens. "My, they sure are cute, Joe." Andy hung over
the kittens. "I wish I had one. Couldn't you give me
just one, Joe?"

"No sirree, Andy. I want every single one. Boy, am
I lucky!"

"Hi, boys!" Aunt Minnie drove up in her buggy. "Are you
going to the big circus tomorrow?"

"Sure am!" Joe called. "Pa's going to take me. We've got
money for a front-row seat. You going, Andy?"

"Dunno yet," Andy put his hands into his jeans. Not a penny
in his pocket. There wasn't much money in his house.
He shuffled his feet and whistled a little tune.

"Better scratch up some cash and go, Andy," Aunt Minnie
called as she drove away. "It's going to be a humdinger!"

"Well, maybe I can." Andy waved good-bye. Then he
pushed off. "So long," he said to Joe. "Got to get on; this
ice is melting!" He pedaled on.

Mildred lived in the next house. Mildred was pretty and she
thought everything Andy did was tops. As Andy came near
he took his hands off the handlebars and rode "no hands."
He pretended not to see Mildred running toward him.

"Oh, Andy!" she called.

Andy stopped.

"Did you see the circus picture, Andy? I'm going, and I'm going to take Miss Melissa!"

"Who's Miss Melissa?"

"My doll, of course. I'm making her a new dress to wear. Are you going to the circus, Andy?"

"Oh, sure!" Andy said grandly. "I'm going to be a clown when I'm grown up. I have to go to get ideas for my clown act."

"Oh, Andy, how wonderful!"

"Well, I've got to get this ice home. So long, Mildred!"

Andy rode on. "Gee, I've just got to get a ticket to that circus! If I'm not there, what will Mildred think?"

Near Bill's house he heard a shout, and Bill came running across the potato field. "Hey, Andy, wait. Look what I've got. I caught him in the ditch!"

Andy slowed down. Bill put his hand into his pocket and brought out a large bullfrog.

"Boy, is he a jumper! Our scout troop is having a frog race tomorrow. If this baby doesn't win that race, I'll eat my shoes!"

"He's a big one, all right." Andy examined the frog.

"Just watch him." Bill set the frog on the path. For a moment it sat staring. Its big eyes bulged. Then it made a jump, then another and another.

"Look at him go," yelled Andy.

"He's a champion!" cried Bill.

"Watch out!" cried Andy. "He's headed for the potato vines. If he gets in there, you'll never find him."

Bill made a grab for his frog. He snatched, he pounced, but the frog was too quick for him. Andy went grabbing too, but it was no use. With one last jump into the potato patch, the frog was lost.

The boys lifted the big leaves. Up one row and down another they went. They peered and peered, but the frog was nowhere to be seen.

Finally Andy gave up. "I've got to get along. Ma's ice is melting fast. Sure am sorry about your jumper, Bill."

"Yea." Bill looked downhearted. "He was good enough to be in the circus." Then all of a sudden he looked cheerful. "Well anyway, I'm going to the circus. It's a big one. You going, Andy?"

"I'm thinking about it." Andy looked down. He scuffed one foot in the dust, then he got onto his bike. "So long, Bill!"

He rode along feeling low. How could he get the money to go to the circus? He remembered that Mom sometimes had a little money. She saved it from selling eggs. He'd seen her putting it into a coffee can in the kitchen.

"I'll ask Mom," he thought, and felt more cheerful. "Maybe she'll give me the money." He pedaled on, whistling.

On the road ahead he caught sight of his friend Jeff. Trotting beside him was Sukey, his pet pig. Andy perked up. Jeff was fun—he had a yard full of pets!

"Hi, Andy!" Jeff opened his front gate. "Come see, I've taught Sukey a new trick!"

Andy put his hat over the ice to shade it. Then he followed Jeff into his back yard. There were the animals all eating supper.

"Now just watch!" Jeff set Sukey on top of a basketball. Then he put an apple on her head. She sat straight up and the apple stayed put.

"Gee!" Andy exclaimed. "Sukey's a bright little pig!"

14

Jeff's mother was on the back porch. "Sure she is," she agreed. "But she's eating us out of house and home. Why, the corn that pig eats would keep two orphans alive. Jeff has got to get rid of some of this zoo. That pig goes first."

Jeff laughed. "She's always saying that," he said to Andy. "Don't worry, she doesn't mean it."

Andy looked at Jeff's mother. Maybe she did mean it— she looked fretted.

"Got to shove along now." He put on his hat and climbed onto his bike.

"See you at the circus!" Jeff waved him good-bye.

When Andy got home, his dog, Dukie, came barking and begging for a ride on the platform.

"No room this time, Dukie." Andy rode around to the back. He lifted out the block of ice and took it into the kitchen. Mom was there waiting.

"My goodness, it's melted half away," she said as Andy put
it into the old icebox. "I'll be glad when I can buy a
refrigerator. Those things make their own ice. It's like
a miracle. You don't have to haul in ice every day!"

"Boy, that would be great!" Andy said.

"I've been saving and saving to buy one," Ma said.
"Every extra penny I put into that coffee can. I counted the
money today. A few more dollars and I'll have it!"

Andy's spirits sank. How could he ask Mom for money when she needed every penny to buy a refrigerator? He got a cracker for Dukie and wandered sadly onto the back porch.

"Sit!" Andy said and tossed the cracker. Dukie caught it in his mouth. "Good boy!" Dukie could learn tricks, too!

At the barn, Andy could see Pop taking the harness off the mule. Maybe he would give him the circus money!

"I'll go ask Pop." He wheeled the plow point to the barn.

"I'm sure glad to get this," Pop said as he lifted off the point. "This old mule had slow work today with that dull point."

Andy was just about to ask for the circus money when Pop said, "I'm saving up to buy a tractor. Just think, Andy, with a tractor I can plow six rows at a time. I can raise a lot more cotton, make a lot more money. Every penny I can spare I put into the bank for our tractor."

Andy's face fell. It didn't seem right to ask Pop for money when he was saving to buy a tractor. He scuffed and scuffed his feet, thinking about the circus. "Nope, I can't ask Pop for his tractor money." He felt downhearted.

"Well," he said to Pop. "I'd better take Grandpa his candy."
He ran along the path that led across the fields to Grandpa's.

"Maybe Gramps will have some money," he thought.
"Maybe he'll buy me a ticket." Andy's hopes rose.

He found Grandpa in the front yard mowing the lawn.
Sitting on a limb of the apple tree was Blackie, his pet crow.

"Corn, corn, corn!" Blackie cawed as Andy entered the yard.

Grandpa stopped his work. "It's all he thinks of—corn," he
complained. "Most crows can learn to talk a little. But this
one doesn't want to learn, he only wants to holler 'corn'!
Well, boy, did you bring my horehound?"

"Sure did, Gramps!" Andy held out the bag.

"Thanks, son." Grandpa put it into his pocket. "When I get
through mowing I'll sit down and have a treat. You have
some?"

"Thanks." Andy took some candy. "Say, Gramps, are you
saving to buy a power mower?" he asked.

"Nope," Grandpa replied. "Pushing this mower keeps my joints from getting rusty. Don't want any of these newfangled gadgets that run by themselves. Rather do things with my own hands."

"Well, Gramps, if you're not saving your money for anything, could you buy me a circus ticket?"

"Great snakes, boy, don't go bothering people for money. If you want a ticket to the circus, go to the circus grounds and get yourself a job. They'll pay you with a ticket to the big show."

Andy's ears stood out. "A job—on the circus grounds—what kind of a job?"

"Lots of things a boy can do. Water the elephants, curry down the zebras, pull the ropes that hoist the big tent. Takes a lot of boys to pull that tent up."

"Honest, Gramps, you think I could get a job like that?"

"Why, sure. But you'll have to get there early, right after sunup. Once they get the tent up, it'll be too late. They don't want any kids around after that. They'll be busy then getting dressed for the big parade."

"Golly, Gramps, thanks. I'll try it!"

Andy bounded along home. He told Mom and Pop of his plan. They both thought it was a fine idea.

Andy hurried through his chores. He emptied the drip pan under the icebox. He gave the mule eight ears of corn and some hay. That night he went to bed early. He was almost too excited to sleep, but at last he dropped off. When he awoke the roosters were crowing—the sun would soon be up. He got up in a hurry and jumped into his clothes.

He ran down to the kitchen. Mom was there rushing around. "I've already fixed your breakfast," she said and put a plate of hot cornbread and a slice of fried ham on the table.

"I'll eat going along." Andy made a bread-and-ham sandwich and took a huge bite. He hurried out and jumped on his bike.

"Hey, Andy, wait!" Mom came running. "Take this watermelon to your grandma in town. She's sick in bed. It'll tempt her to eat."

"Sure will, Mom!"

Mom put the watermelon into the basket. Andy gave a push with his foot and he was off. He was whizzing through the gate when he heard someone shouting. He looked back. There, running after him, was Gramps with Blackie, the crow.

"Hey, Andy!" Grandpa shouted. "Wait a minute!"

Andy braked the bike and Grandpa came hurrying. "Here, boy, take this pesky bird clean away!"

"Gramps! What's the matter—you want to get rid of Blackie?"

"Sure do. Can't get my sleep with this bird around. Comes sitting on my window every morning. Wakes me up at the crack of dawn. 'Corn, corn, corn!' he starts a-cawing before it's light."

"But—but what'll I do with him?"

"I don't care. Well, give him to your Aunt Minnie. She's always saying it's hard to wake up mornings. He'll fix that."

"But Gramps, I can't carry him; he'll fly away."

"No, he won't. I've got a lead sinker tied to his foot. He'll sit right here on your hat. Get along now, or you'll be late."

Andy rode away with the crow on his hat. He'd hardly gone a half mile when he heard a barking behind him. He looked back. There was Dukie running after him. Andy's heart sank. He'd forgotten to shut the gate.

"Go home, Dukie!" he shouted. It would not do to have Dukie follow to the circus grounds. An elephant might step on him, or maybe he'd go sniffing into the lion's cage. "Dukie, go home!"

Dukie paid no mind. He ran on, barking. Andy slowed down. There was only one thing to do. "Come, Dukie, have a ride!"

Dukie came bounding. Andy lifted him and set him on the back platform. Sitting there, he'd be out of mischief.

Andy pedaled on as fast as he could. He was soon in sight of Jeff's house. There was Jeff sneaking through the gate. He kept looking back over his shoulder.

"I wonder what's the matter?" Andy thought. Jeff acts like something is after him. And there, he's got Sukey on the end of a rope. That's funny. Sukey always follows. She doesn't need any rope!"

Once on the road, Jeff began to run so fast that Sukey could not keep up. Jeff dragged her along.

Andy rode fast and overtook them. "Hey, Jeff, what's happened? Why all the hurry?"

"Oh, Andy," Jeff panted. "Ma and Pa have decided to sell Sukey. The man's coming for her right away. They say he'll only put her in the woods to eat acorns, but I'm afraid he'll take her to the butcher."

"To the butcher!" Andy's eyes bulged. His bike wobbled. "A pretty little pig, a smart little pig like Sukey! Can't you hide her, Jeff?"

"No time!" Jeff peered behind. "Here comes the man!"

Andy looked. Down the road came a truck stirring up dust.

"Quick, Andy!" Jeff cried. "Put Sukey in your basket and get her away!"

"But the basket's full, you can see. I've got a melon for Grandma. She's sick."

"Sukey can sit on the melon. Easy as pie."

"But I'm going to the circus grounds to get a job. What'll I do with her?"

"Get her a job too. Any clown would be glad to get Sukey. She can do tricks."

"Well . . ." Andy looked back. The truck was almost on them. "Heft her up, Jeff."

Quickly Jeff lifted Sukey. He gave her a kiss on her little pink snout. "Sit right there, Sukey-baby. You'll have fun with the circus."

Sukey grunted affectionately. "Oink, oink, oink."

Andy gave a push. Gosh, the bike was getting heavy! He got it rolling and pedaled away.

He had just passed Bill's potato patch when he heard a shout. "Andy! Hey, Andy!"

He looked around. There was Bill's mother on the porch.
"I just caught him!" she cried, and held up a long-legged
bullfrog. "In the potato patch. Put my hand in to scrabble out
a potato and felt something clammy. It scared me almost
to death—I thought it was a snake. But no, it was Bill's
jumper."

"Must be him," Andy agreed.

"Say, Andy, can't you take him to Bill? He's gone to town
for the jumping-frog race. They're having it early, so the
boys can go to the circus parade. Bill was awfully put out
about losing his frog. He searched and searched yesterday.
Didn't give up till sundown. Do take him along, Andy."

"How can I carry him, Mrs. Jones? He'll jump away!"

"Oh." Mrs. Jones looked worried. "That's so." Then she
brightened. "I've got an idea!" She rushed into the house and
brought an ice cube. She popped it into the frog's mouth.

"He won't jump now, Andy," she assured him. "Frogs don't
jump when they're cold. Frogs hardly move when they're
cold. They sleep all winter. With that ice in his mouth he'll
think it's cold wintertime. He'll snooze the whole way to
town. When he gets there, Bill can take the ice out of his
mouth. He'll warm up and be as lively as ever."

"But where can I put him?"

"Why, right here on Sukey's head. She does tricks, doesn't
she? She can hold a frog on her head."

"Well, all right, Mrs. Jones. I'll try."

Mrs. Jones set the frog on Sukey's head. There he sat
goggling straight ahead. Andy started to push off.

"Wait, Andy. Do take these. The scoutmaster asked Bill to
bring some baby frogs to show the boys. Bill was so upset
about losing his fancy jumper, he forgot." She held out a jar.

30

"Baby frogs? They don't look like frogs!"

"But they are. They're tadpoles. They'll grow feet and drop their tails and then they're frogs."

"Oh, gee, Mrs. Jones. I can't carry a jar of tadpoles!"

"Shucks, Andy, I've seen you riding 'no hands' lots of times. Hold the jar in your left hand. It's not far."

"Well, I'll try." Andy took the jar and rode on.

Up ahead was Mildred's house, and there was Mildred
running down the walk. She had her doll, Miss Melissa,
in her arms.

"Andy, wait!" she cried. "Where are you going, Andy?"

Andy put out his right hand and caught hold of the gate.
"Going to the circus grounds to get a job."

"A job—how great! Oh, Andy, can't you take Miss Melissa?"

"Miss Melissa—your doll?" Andy was shocked.

"Yes, my doll. Here she is, all dressed up. I promised to
take her myself, but Mama won't let me. Miss Melissa is
terribly disappointed. She feels like crying."

Tears began to roll from Mildred's eyes. They made Andy

feel upset. "But where can I put a doll? Looks like
I'm loaded."

"Let her sit here." Mildred took Blackie away and made a
dent in Andy's hat. "From here she can see everything."

"But what about Grandpa's crow?"

"He can sit right here." Mildred set Blackie on top of
Miss Melissa's head. Blackie fluttered his wings and tried to
take off, but the lead sinker was too heavy for him.

"Thank you, Andy. Miss Melissa will never forget this."

"Oh, that's all right. I'm glad to help out. 'By, Mildred, I've
got to hurry." Andy squinted at the sun. Its rim was shining
above pink clouds. It was getting late.

Andy pedaled on. "Gosh, I hope nobody else is in trouble."

No such luck. Up ahead he saw Joe running toward him. He was carrying something in his hat.

"Oh, Andy, wait. Something awful—"

Andy slowed down, then put a foot to the ground to stop himself.

"I heard Papa—" Joe said, out of breath. "He told Mama he was going to the mill to get some corn ground. Mama said, 'Well, take those kittens. We can't have a house full of cats.'"

"What did she mean by that?" Andy asked.

"There's a millpond. Maybe Papa will throw my kittens into the millpond."

Andy was horrified. He peered into Joe's hat. The baby cats looked up at him.

"Can't you save my kittens, Andy? Take 'em with you, Andy!"

"But I'm going to get a job on the circus grounds. What'll I do with six kittens?" Andy cried.

"Give 'em to your Aunt Minnie. She hasn't got any children, hasn't even got a husband. She'll be glad to have all these little cats. Hurry, Andy, there's Papa. He's hunting for 'em."

Andy looked. Joe's Papa was peering under the house, into the hen's nests, every which way. "How can I carry six kittens?" he exclaimed. "There's no place to put 'em."

"Put 'em under your hat, Andy!"

"All right, Joe. Stuff 'em under. But make it quick.
I've got to get to the circus in a hurry. If I get there after the
sun's high, I won't get a job. And look—it's climbing."

Hurriedly, Joe lifted one side of Andy's hat.

"Watch out!" Andy cried. "Don't upset Miss Melissa."

Joe shoved some of the kittens into the crown of the hat,
others he stuffed into Andy's pocket.

"Thank you, Andy. I'll do something for you someday."

"That's all right, Joe." Andy glanced toward the barn.
Joe's father was hurrying toward them. Andy stepped hard
on the pedals and streaked away. He could feel the kittens
crawling on the top of his head. It gave him the jitters.
"Well," he comforted himself, "it's not far to Aunt
Minnie's house."

He was there in no time. "Oh, Auntie!" he called. Aunt
Minnie waved. "Auntie, come quick; I've got a present
for you!"

Aunt Minnie came rushing out, a pie in one hand.

"Grandpa has sent you a present," Andy called.

"A present? Why, how sweet of Grandpa!" Aunt Minnie
looked pleased. "What is it?"

"It's Blackie here, his pet crow."

"Oh . . . Blackie . . ." Aunt Minnie's voice went way down.

"He says Blackie will keep you from sleeping too late.
He'll get you up mornings."

"Oh, no, he won't!" cried Aunt Minnie. "I'm not going to have that croaking critter. Grandpa can't put him off on me. You tell him I don't want his present!"

"But Aunt Minnie," Andy exclaimed. "I'm on my way to the circus grounds. I can't take this crow!"

"Well, you can't leave him here; that's flat!" Aunt Minnie started into the house.

Andy was upset. He felt the kittens scrabbling and squirming on top of his head.

"Aunt Minnie, wait. Here's something else for you."

Aunt Minnie turned. "Another present?" She looked sour.

"Yes, but you'll like this one. It's cute and pretty. From Joe, down the road."

"Now why would Joe be sending me a present? It's probably something he doesn't want."

"Oh, no, Aunt Minnie. He loves it. It . . . they're six little kittens, Aunt Minnie."

Aunt Minnie screamed. "And my old mother cat with seven already! Don't say another word. Go along with your presents. No! Wait. I've got one for you." She held out the pie. "It's for Grandma. Take it along to her."

"Aunt Minnie!" cried Andy. "Where would I put a pie?"

"Hold it in your right hand, Andy. I've seen you riding 'no hands' many a time. It's only a little way down the road." She set the pie in Andy's hand.

"And look, here's my little dickey-bird. Take him along too; he'll cheer Grandma up. And wait, here's her sewing basket."

"Aunt Minnie," cried Andy. "I can't take all these things!"

"Why, sure you can, Andy. Here, take the sewing basket in your left hand along with the tadpoles." She slipped the handle over his fingers. "And now you can carry the bird cage on your right shoulder. Here." She slid it onto his arm.

"Now get ready. I'll give you a shove. You'll make it!"

"Oh, gee!" And sat up straight, trying to balance everything. Aunt Minnie gave him a mighty push, and he was off. At first he wobbled a little, then he got going and rode fast. The sun was high now and shining brightly.

"If I take time to get these things to Grandma now," Andy thought, "I'll never make it in time for a job."

Up ahead he saw the gate to the circus grounds. Flags were flying over the top. He could hear men shouting. Animals were trumpeting and roaring. Things were getting under way.

"It's now or never," thought Andy.

Leaning this way and that to stay up, Andy rode through the gate. His hopes sank—there was the big tent already up. Flags were fluttering. All the circus people were dressed and ready for the big parade. He was too late. Too late to get a job. Too late to earn a ticket to the big show. Andy was heartsick. His bike wobbled this way and that. He saw the circus people staring, the Ringmaster in a red coat, the spangled ladies, the clowns. Then he felt his front wheel going

over a stone—and—slip, slide—skid—down he went
with everything!

The clowns ran to help, but Dukie barked at them and
scared them away. Andy sat up. Oh, what a terrible mess!
He began to cry.

The Ringmaster helped him up. "Don't cry, sonny; nobody's
hurt," he said. "We'll catch all your livestock. We'll get you
another watermelon, too."

"But—but now it's too late. I wanted a job," sobbed Andy.

"A job?" asked the Ringmaster. "With the circus?"

"Yes, sir," Andy replied. "I—I got up at daybreak. I meant
to get here early, but people kept asking me to take things.
It slowed me down."

"Well now, let me see," said the Ringmaster. "Maybe we can give you a job after all."

Andy stopped crying. "Do you think so? What could I do?"

"How would you like to be a clown?"

"A clown?" Andy's eyes popped open. "In the big show?"

"That's right."

"But—but I wouldn't know what to do. I wouldn't know how to be funny."

"Why, sonny," said the Ringmaster. "You have just put on the funniest act I ever saw. See how everybody is laughing."

Andy looked around. The spangled ladies, the men in fancy costumes, even the clowns were rocking with laughter.

"Couldn't you ride around the ring and fall down again just like you did a minute ago?"

Andy wiped the tears with the back of his hand. "Why sure, that would be easy." He grinned.

"You're hired!" said the Ringmaster. "You're going to be a clown in the big show—for the whole summer!"

Andy was overjoyed. He could hardly believe his good luck. "I'll have to ask my folks," he said.

"You go home and ask 'em. Here are free tickets for everybody. Come right back and we'll get you ready for the show."

Andy took off. By the time the parade was over he was back. Mom and Pop had said yes. They were pleased he would have a chance to see the country, and earn some money too.

The Ringmaster took him to the dressing tent. The clowns painted his face and gave him a pair of big shoes.

When the show opened that afternoon, how surprised Andy's friends were—there he was riding around the ring! They thought his act was the funniest of all, the very best part of the show.

So when the circus train left the next morning, they were all there to tell him good-bye.

Mildred handed him a little valise.

"Here are Miss Melissa's clothes," she called. "What a wonderful trip she'll have!"

"Hey, Andy!" cried Bill. "Put froggie where there are lots of flies. He eats flies."

"Boy!" cried Jeff, who was there with his parents. "Think of Sukey doing tricks for the circus. Gee!"

"Here's something for you, Andy." Aunt Minnie handed up a pie. "This one is to eat."

"Good-bye, good-bye!" Mom stood waving. "Don't forget to brush your teeth every day."

Pop called out, "When you get back, I'll have that tractor. Times will be better."

The train began to move. "Remember what I said, boy!" shouted Grandpa. "Don't go bothering folks about money. Get yourself a job. It's more fun that way."

"Good-bye, good-bye!" Andy waved back. Then the circus train pulled out.

ELLIS CREDLE was brought up in North Carolina on the coast just across from Hatteras Island. Her ancestors had settled in the vicinity in the earliest days, when the state was a British colony, and family members have been there ever since. She taught school in the Blue Ridge Mountains of North Carolina, from which she draws the background for many of her books. She lived in New York for a number of years, during which she studied at the Art Students League and at the New York School of Interior Decoration; she also worked at the Brooklyn Children's Museum and at the American Museum of Natural History. In 1947 she and her husband and son moved to Mexico, where they have lived ever since. She is the author of over twenty books for children, including the modern classic DOWN, DOWN THE MOUNTAIN.

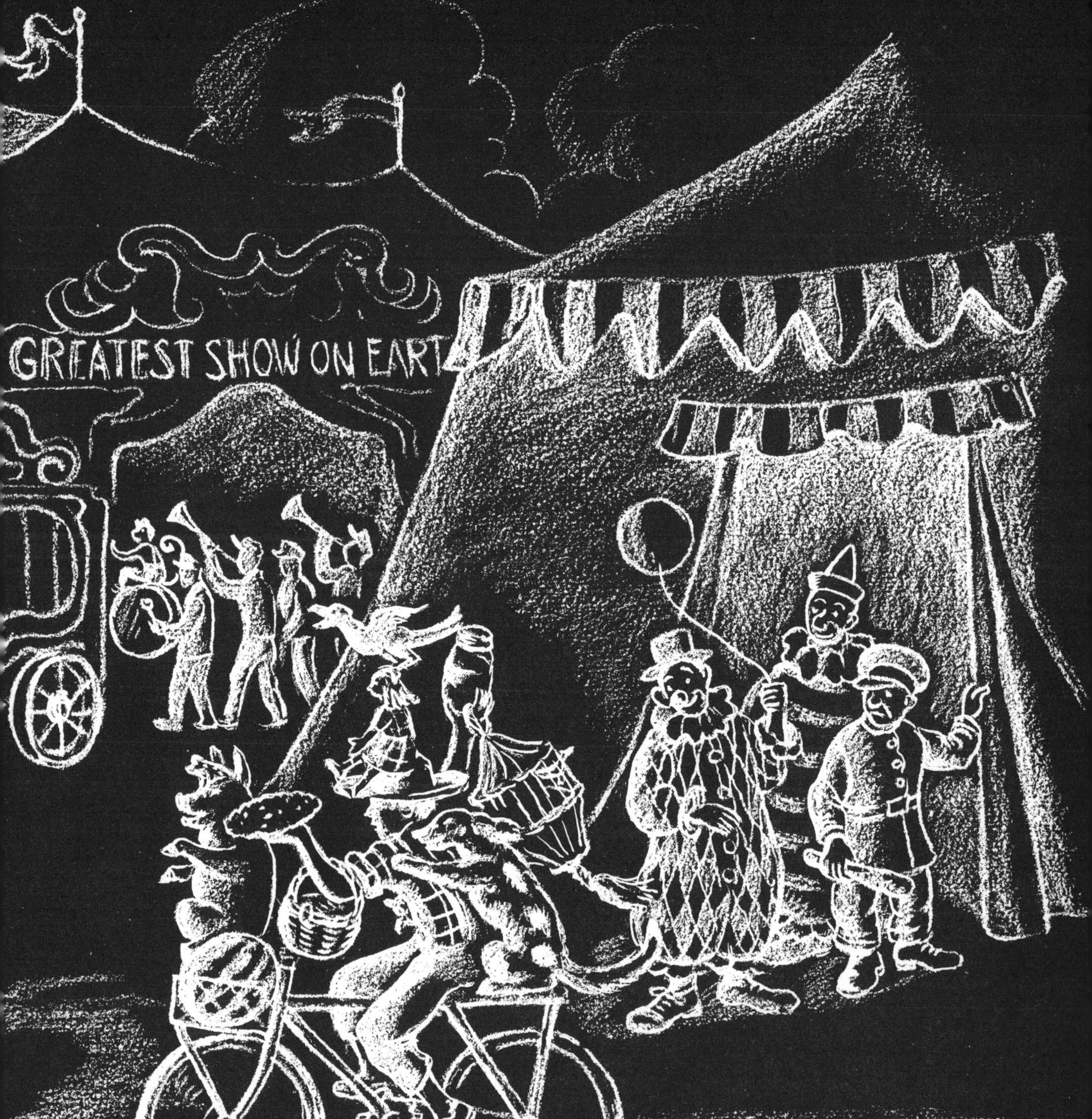
GREATEST SHOW ON EART

Credle

X(3)

45356

DATE DUE

9-9-07	Broken Bow PL	JUN 2 2 2015
MAY 1 5 2008		
9-16-09	Lincoln City	
10-24-09	Lincoln City	
JUN 2 5 2012		
	Crawford PL	
3-12-14	Norfolk PL	
10-8-14	Lincoln P.L.	
JAN 2 2 2015		